TALES FROM
THE BACK
PEW

THE THREE
WISE GUYS

written by **Mike Thaler** illustrated by **Jared Lee**

ZONDERkidz

ZONDERVAN.com/
AUTHORTRACKER
follow your favorite authors

To
Mrs. Hankemeier
and all the kids
at Abiding Savior Lutheran School
St. Louis
—M.T., J.L.

ZONDERKIDZ

The Three Wise Guys
Copyright © 2010 by Mike Thaler
Illustrations © 2010 by Jared Lee Studio, Inc.

Requests for information should be addressed to:

Zondervan, *Grand Rapids, Michigan 49530*

Library of Congress Cataloging-in-Publication Data

Thaler, Mike, 1936-
    The three wise guys / by Mike Thaler ; illustrated by Jared Lee.
       p. cm. — (Tales from the back pew)
    Summary: A wise-cracking boy is recruited to play one of the wise men in the
Christmas pageant.
    ISBN 978-0-310-71593-1 (softcover : saddle stitch)
    [1. Christmas—Fiction. 2. Pageants Fiction. 3. Christian life—Fiction.
4. Humorous stories.] I. Lee, Jared D., ill. II. Title.
    PZ7.T3Tk 2010
    [E]—dc22   2008038672

Editor: Mary Hassinger
Art Director: Merit Kathan

Printed in China

10 11 12 13 14 /LPC/ 22 21 20 19 18 17 16 15 14 13 12 11 10 9 8 7 6 5 4 3 2 1

The kids at our church are putting on a Christmas pageant. They asked me if I'd like to be a part from the play. I said, "Yes, I would like to be apart from the play."

They asked me if I'd like to be on the stage.
"Yes," I answered, "the first stage out of town."

My Sunday school teacher didn't think that was so funny, so he gave me a part anyway. I'm one of the three wise guys.

He says that will be a good part for me.

We're called the Three Magpies, or something like that.
In the play we rent camels from a Camelot and set out to find baby Jesus.

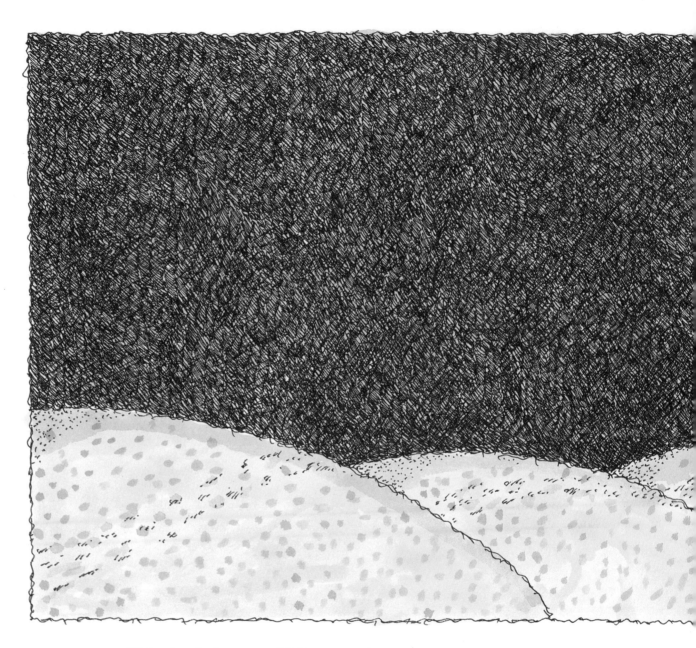

We don't have a GPS so we bring our own star.

MAP → GPS → STAR → ☆ COMPASS →

Anyway, we stop at a tourist information booth to get directions. That's where I have my speaking part.

I get to say, "Where is the one who has been born King of the Jews? We saw His star in the east and have come to worship Him."

Unfortunately, the guy working the desk that day is King Hair-odd, who's having a bad heir day. He is so jealous of competition he won't even let a Burger King into town.

He doesn't know where the baby is, but he'd like to find him too.
Secretly, he plans to follow us and eliminate the competition.

Well, we're wise men, so we outsmart him.
My Sunday school teacher says we're really three smart alecs.

So anyway, we follow the star to a manger,
where Mary is hugging a Cabbage Patch doll.

We pretend it's the real baby Jesus and bow down,
offering gifts of gold, Frankenstein, and myrrh. Whatever that is.

Then we get up and hit the road. But I have a dream that tells us to avoid Hair-odd's information booth, so we go home a different way.

But Hair-odd finds out anyway and goes to Bethlehem
to cause some heir-raising trouble.

But God is smarter than everybody and sends Joseph and Mary to Egypt, which saves the baby Jesus.

So E-gyps Hair-odd out of his scheme and saves his son so that He can grow up and save us.

In the play, we followed the star to Jesus. But I really feel like a wise man, for every day I follow the star of Jesus, who is the light of the world.

Whoever serves me must follow me.
—John 12:26